# Bink & gollie

## Best Friends For Ever

Kate DiCamillo and Alison McGhee

illustrated by Tony Fucile

WALKER BOOKS
AND SUBSIDIARIES
LONDON · BOSTON · SYDNEY · AUCKLAND

For Jennifer Roberts, tallest of them all

K. D.


For Charlie Anken, loved and missed

A. M.


For Stacey, my best friend for ever

T. F.

First published in paperback 2014 by Walker Books Ltd
87 Vauxhall Walk, London SE11 5HJ

2 4 6 8 10 9 7 5 3 1

Text © 2013 Kate DiCamillo and Alison McGhee
Illustrations © 2013 Tony Fucile

The right of Kate Di Camillo, Alison McGhee and Tony Fucile to be identified
as authors and illustrator respectively of this work has been asserted by them
in accordance with the Copyright, Designs and Patents Act 1988

This book has been typeset in Humana Sans

Printed in China

British Library Cataloguing in Publication Data:
a catalogue record for this book is available from the British Library

ISBN 978-1-4063-4495-0

www.walker.co.uk

# Contents

# Empire

## of

# Enchantment

"I have long suspected that royal blood flowed in my veins," said Gollie.

Aunt Natasha
Sept. 21, 1908

"Good news, Bink," said Gollie. "I have made an extraordinary discovery."

"I'll be right over," said Bink.

"Good news almost always means pancakes," said Bink.

"Bring on the pancakes," said Bink.

"Pancakes?" said Gollie. "What pancakes?"

"The good-news pancakes," said Bink.

"Bink," said Gollie, "you must stop thinking with your stomach. Look."

"Who's that?" said Bink.

"That," said Gollie, "is my great-aunt Natasha. As you can see, she was a queen."

"All righty, then," said Bink. "Let's eat!"

"I shall no longer be cooking pancakes for you, Bink," said Gollie.

"Why not?" said Bink.

"I regret to inform you," said Gollie, "that royalty does not cook for others."

"Oh," said Bink. "OK. I regret to inform you that I am going home."

Aunt Natasha
Sept. 21, 1908

"I look like my true self," said Gollie.

"Very well, then," said Gollie. "I shall go forth into my kingdom alone."

"A remarkable road," said Gollie.

"The queen thanks you for your efforts on behalf of the empire. Carry on."

"Lovely onions," said Gollie. "Pungent in the extreme. The queen does love a good onion. Carry on."

"Mr Eccles. Mrs Eccles," said Gollie. "You may be interested to know that I, too, find myself in possession of an empire."

"May peace reign over both of our empires," said Gollie.

"Knock, knock," said Gollie.

"Who's there?" said Bink.

"The queen," said Gollie.

"I'm still not home," said Bink.

"The Kingdom of Gollie has grown muddy," said Gollie.

"The crown grows heavy," said Gollie.

"The queen is lonely," said Gollie.

"Knock, knock," said Gollie.

"Who's there?" said Bink.

"It's me," said Gollie. "Gollie."

"Gollie," said Bink. "I've missed you."

# Why Should You Be Shorter Than Your Friends?

"Could you step aside, Bink?" said Gollie.

"I can reach that, Bink," said Gollie.

"Let me get that for you, Bink," said Gollie.

"That's a good question," said Bink.

"I can't think of a reason," said Bink.

"All righty, then," said Bink. "I will."

# PRECAUTIONS

Excessive assembly required.

Follow instructions closely.

Or else.

© Stretch-O-Matic   ACME IN

ACME INDUSTRIES INC. For the original purchase
year limited warranty covers STRETCH-O-MATIC against
in materials and workmanship. The six-month limited warr
applies to the attachable parts on the main base only. Wear
to the springs is to be expected and any damage will be
considered normal use. This warranty covers normal usage and
does not cover the STRETCH-O-MATIC non-spring parts.
Evidence of any consumer repair will void this warranty.
THIS WARRANTY DOES NOT COVER, AND IS INTENDED
TO EXCLUDE, ANY LIABILITY ON THE PART OF ACME
INDUSTRIES INC., WHETHER UNDER THIS W
OR IMPLIED BY L

"Or else what?" said Bink.

"This Acme Stretch-o-Matic is top quality," said Bink.
"I can feel it working already."

"Hello, Gollie," said Bink. "Notice anything different about me?"

"I do not," said Gollie.

"All righty, then," said Bink. "Back to the Acme Stretch-o-Matic."

"The Acme Stretch-o-Matic?" said Gollie.

"Things are happening now,"
said Bink.

"Are you ready to be astonished, Gollie?" said Bink. "A dramatic change has occurred. You won't want to miss this. Act now!"

"Oh, dear," said Gollie.

KNOCK, KNOCK!

"Come in!" said Bink.

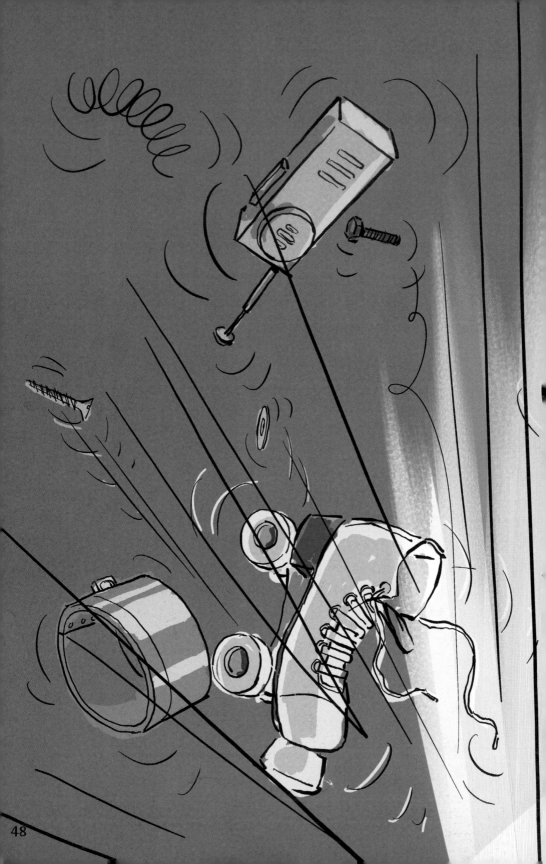

"Bink," said Gollie, "I fear that it will be well-nigh impossible
to reconstruct the Stretch-o-Matic."

"Now hand me some peanut butter," said Bink.

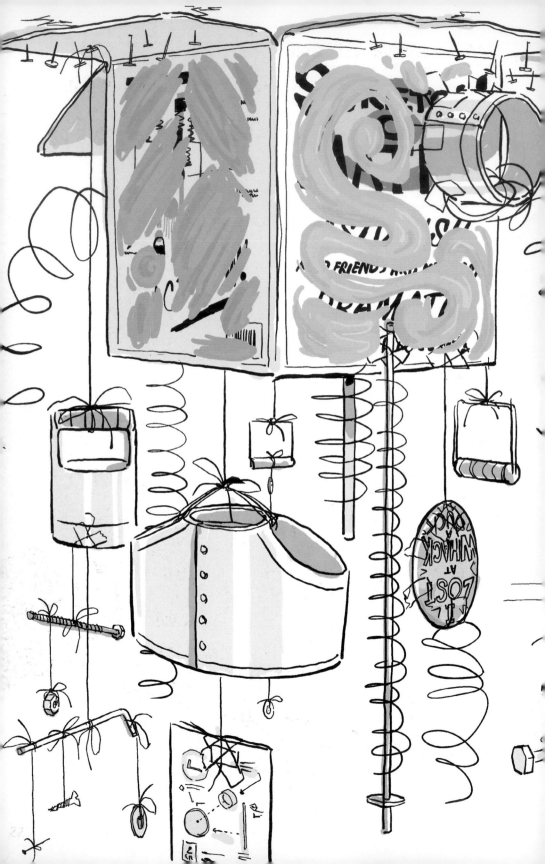

"Astonishing," said Gollie.

"It makes me feel taller just to look at it," said Bink.

"Art can have that effect," said Gollie.

INVENTOR OF PEANUT BUTTER

# Kudos,
# Bink
# and
# Gollie

"Look, Bink," said Gollie. "Here is Edna O'Dell and her collection of international garden gnomes."

"Hmm," said Bink.

"Look," said Gollie. "Here is the world's largest ball of tin foil. How very interesting."

"Hmm," said Bink.

"Look," said Gollie. "'Pictured here is Mr Jerome Gardner of Freeport, New York, sitting with a few million of the marbles in his ever-growing collection. Good work, Jerome.'"

"Hmm," said Bink.

"Maybe we should collect something," said Bink.

"Excellent idea, Bink," said Gollie. "Then we, too, could have our photo in *Flicker's Arcana*."

"But what should we collect?" said Bink.

"Surely we can find something at Eccles' Empire of Enchantment," said Gollie.

"Help you?" said Mr Eccles.

"Help you?" said Mrs Eccles.

"Yes," said Gollie. "We would like to start a collection."

"We're going to become world-record-holders and get our picture in this book," said Bink.

"You've got your decorative thimbles," said Mrs Eccles. "You've got your rings made out of spoons."

"I like gold star stickers," said Bink. "Let's start with gold star stickers."

"Aisle ten," said Mr Eccles.

"Aisle ten," said Mrs Eccles.

"One hundred packets of sixty-six stars each makes six thousand, six hundred gold star stickers," said Bink. "No one in the entire world could possibly have more gold star stickers than that. We're winners."

"Bink," said Gollie, "I have just made a disturbing discovery. Look: 'Pictured here is Celeste Pascal of Petaluma, California, standing in front of her bungalow, which is entirely covered in gold star stickers. Kudos, Celeste.'"

"Kudos?" said Bink.

"Kudos means congratulations," said Gollie.

"That looks like more than six thousand, six
hundred gold stars," said Bink.

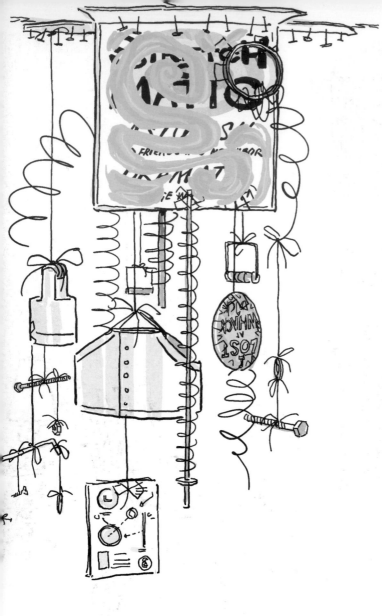

"We don't have a bungalow entirely covered in gold star stickers," said Gollie.

"And we don't have a million marbles," said Bink. "Flicker's will never come to take our photo."

"I can think of someone who would take our photo,"
said Gollie.

"Say cheese," said Mr Eccles.

"Cheese," said Mrs Eccles.

## About the creators

**Kate DiCamillo** is the author of the best-selling *The Magician's Elephant* and the multiple award-winners *The Tale of Despereaux* and *Because of Winn-Dixie*, and the creator of the award-winning Mercy Watson series. Kate DiCamillo lives in Minneapolis, USA.

**Alison McGhee** is the award-winning author of *The Song of Middle C*; Snap; the number 1 bestseller *Someday*; and the young adult novel *All Rivers Flow to the Sea*. Alison McGhee lives in Minnesota and Vermont, USA.

**Tony Fucile** has spent more than twenty years designing and animating characters for cartoon feature films, including *The Lion King* and *The Incredibles*, for which he was a supervising animator. His other picture-book titles include *Let's Do Nothing* and *Driving to Bed*. Tony Fucile lives in San Francisco, USA.

Find out more about Bink and Gollie and their creators at
www.binkandgollie.com

# Praise for *Bink & Gollie*

978-1-4063-3901-7

## A World Book Day "Recommended Read" for 2011

★ "An exceptional book for early readers"

— Sarah Webb, *Irish Independent*

★ "With deliciously spare text and delightful cartoons … wonderfully entertaining."

— *Lovereading4kids.co.uk*

★ "You'd have to have a heart of stone not to be hypnotized by the sheer charm of these stories."

— *School Library Journal*

★ "Oh, happiness! Move over Pippi Longstocking! … Bink and Gollie celebrate the challenges and strengths of a great friendship"

— *New York Times Book Review*

★ "effervescent and endearingly quirky"

— *Wall Street Journal*

# Praise for
## *Bink & Gollie: Two for One*

978-1-4063-4496-7

★ "Utterly chuckle-worthy, charming and (thank goodness) still refreshing." — *Kirkus Reviews*

★ "spot-on ... Kids will be left eagerly anticipating the further adventures of this unlikely – and completely charming – duo" — *Booklist*

★ "plenty of dry comedy and laugh-out-loud comments" — *CBI recommended reads of 2012*

★ "An ideal selection for beginning readers" — *School Library Journal*

★ "Another welcome sequel ... illustrated with zany energy." — *Wall Street Journal*

Available from all good booksellers

www.walker.co.uk